"When the immortal scorer
writes against your name,
he'll write not if you won or lost
but how you played the game."
– a misquote of Grantland Rice

American edition published in 2016 by Andersen Press USA,
an imprint of Andersen Press Ltd.
www.andersenpressusa.com

First published in Great Britain in 2016 by Andersen Press Ltd.,
20 Vauxhall Bridge Road, London SW1V 2SA.

Copyright © David McKee, 2016.

Distributed in the United States and Canada by
Lerner Publishing Group, Inc.
241 First Avenue North
Minneapolis, MN 55401 USA
For reading levels and more information, look up this title at www.lernerbooks.com.

Color separated in Switzerland by Photolitho AG, Zürich.
Printed and bound in China.

Library of Congress Cataloging-in-Publication Data Available.
ISBN: 978-1-5124-1624-4
eBook ISBN: 978-1-5124-1627-5
1-TL-6/1/16

MIX
Paper from
responsible sources
FSC® C104723
FSC
www.fsc.org

ELMER
and the RACE

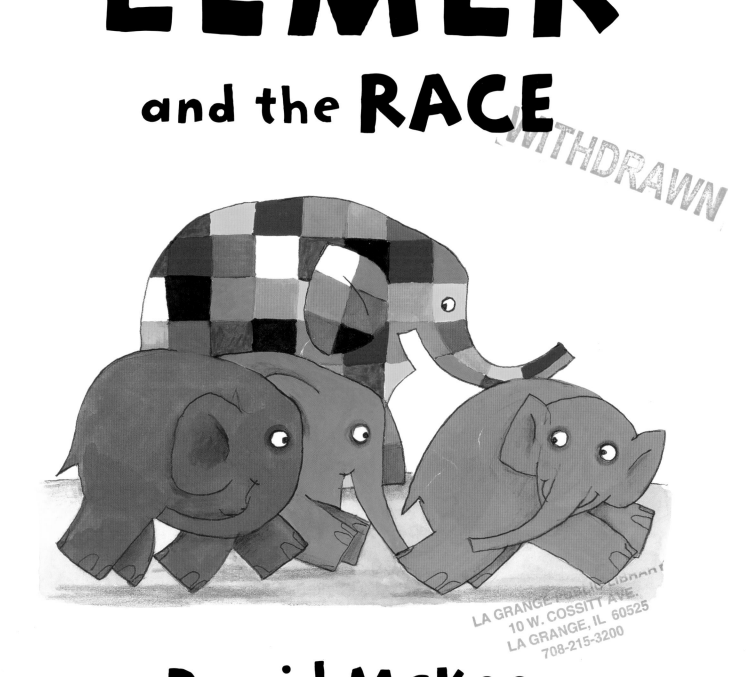

David McKee

Andersen Press USA

Elmer, the patchwork elephant, was walking with his cousin, Wilbur, when a group of noisy young elephants came charging past.

"What's going on?" Elmer asked.

"We were seeing who is the fastest," said one, "and it was me."

"It wasn't, it was me!" said another.

"You both cheated," said a third. "It wasn't a real race."

"Let's have a real race," said Wilbur.

"We need to tell the other animals and decide the course," said Elmer. "We'll have the race next week."

It was a busy, noisy week. The other animals promised to come and watch. There was always one or more of the young elephants practicing and older elephants cheering them on.

On the day, nine elephants showed up ready to race.
Each racer was decorated with a different color.

Blue complained about being blue so Red agreed
to swap with him. Finally they were ready.

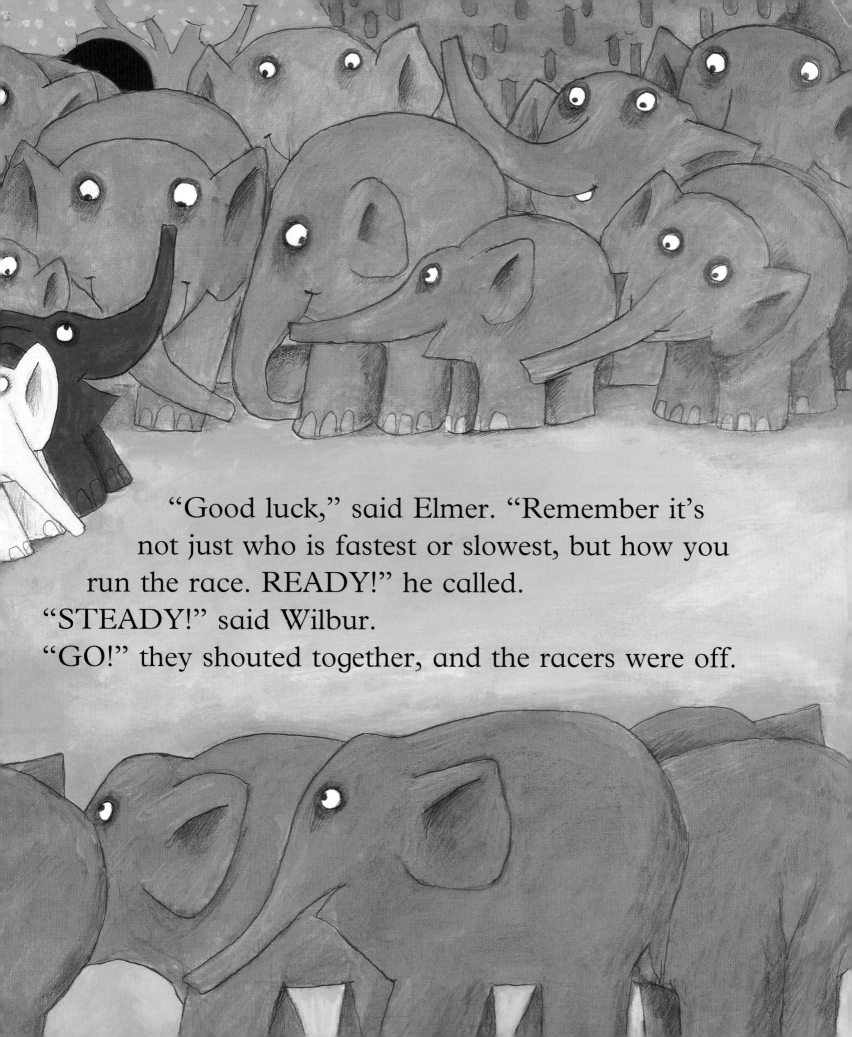

"Good luck," said Elmer. "Remember it's not just who is fastest or slowest, but how you run the race. READY!" he called.

"STEADY!" said Wilbur.

"GO!" they shouted together, and the racers were off.

Elmer and Wilbur had shortcuts to viewing
places along the route. The first was the river—
Brown was there and way ahead of the others.
The crocodiles cheered.
"Brown has started fastest," said Wilbur.
"There's still a long way to go," said Elmer.

Next, it was Monkey Corner. The cheeky monkeys confused the racers by throwing fruit and shouting, "That way!" "No, this way!"

"Faster! Faster! Turn here!"
Pink and Violet went off in the wrong direction while
the others caught up with Brown.

After that, there was a hill.
At the top Yellow was ahead
with Green close behind.
"Pink and Violet are still lost,"
chuckled Elmer.

At Red Rock Valley, Yellow purposefully
tripped Green as she tried to pass.
"Cheat! Cheat!" roared Lion and Tiger.
Green was hurt and White stopped to help her.
"Lucky we saw that," said Wilbur.

Elmer and Wilbur reached the last viewing place
just as Orange prepared to pass Yellow. Yellow
was ready to trip him, as he had Green.
"BOO!" shouted the hippos. Blue saw his chance
and passed them both.
"Yellow is disqualified," said Elmer.

Blue stayed ahead and won.
"That would be me if I hadn't changed color," said Red.
Pink and Violet arrived together, laughing too much to run.

Last was injured Green with White helping her.
Yellow was ashamed and went to say sorry.
"Now for the medals," said Wilbur.

"Well," said Elmer, "Blue gets the medal for finishing first and Orange for finishing second (without a second you can't have a first). There are also medals for the fastest starter, the bravest, the kindest, and the unluckiest. There are two for funniest and one for the sorriest, who used to be the naughtiest. Another day we might have another story. Three cheers for all of you."